JASJ is, without a doubt, the most honest and most hard working person I know. He overcame adversity throughout his life. He is a loving husband and father of two, who are the light of his life. I have never met anyone more dedicated to achieving his goals without lowering his personal standards of honesty, achievement and self-improvement. I wish him great success with his book. I can't wait to read it.

Dr. John Murray,

7344, County 426 M. 5 Rd,

Gladstone, MI 49837.

Last, but far from least, I wish to dedicate this novel to my parents, Mr. J. A. Sami Jayasinghe (father) and Mrs. M. M. Susila Mudalpath (mother) as well as parents of my wife, Mr. H. M. Siriwardane (late father) and Mrs. W. H. Kusumalatha (mother).

JASJ

THIRD JOURNEY

AUSTIN MACAULEY PUBLISHERS™

LONDON • CAMBRIDGE • NEW YORK • SHARJAH

ISBN – 9789948781905 – (Paperback)
ISBN – 9789948781912 – (E-Book)

Application Number: MC-10-01-7990427
Age Classification: 17+

First Published 2023
AUSTIN MACAULEY PUBLISHERS FZE
Sharjah Publishing City
P O Box [519201]
Sharjah, UAE
www.austinmacauley.ae
+971 655 95 202

I wish to express my gratitude to loving wife Mrs. H. M. A. Priyadarshani, elder daughter Ms. J. A. Kavindi Yuhansa Jayasinghe and younger daughter Ms. J. A. Umaya Indeewari Jayasinghe, who generously helped me color the mosaic of this novel with the tiles of their knowledge, expertise and memories.

My grateful special thanks go to Mr. and Mrs. Frank Sri Chandrasekara for their assistance and support on my every effort.

I cannot forget my teachers and lecturers from school to universities.

01

"Brother…wake up! Are you not getting ready to go to school? Time is up!"

The eldest sister, Ayanthi's, daily wakeup call routine not only woke up the younger brother, but also the eldest and the youngest sister with reluctance and complaining.

"Cannot sleep a little more with this harangue of Ayanthi's!"

Ayanthi had already placed the kettle on the fireplace for boiling water to make tea when the mother Suduhamine, habitually said,

"Can you keep the kettle on the fireplace?"

"Today too, the train is late…" That was the father's voice, waking up while hearing the sound of the train far away. As a habit, the father said this although the train may be not be late to arrive.

Mother and Ayanthi were familiar to hear these words of the father in the morning. Sometimes, looking at each other they smiled secretly.

Ayanthi said,

"Brother, your shirt is ironed."

"Sister, now today you are not to get your uniform dirty…"

To elder brother, "Your tea is ready and on the table…"

This was the daily routine for Ayanthi in the mornings.

She performed all this work while also tending to her personal needs.

By 6:10 am, led by elder and younger brothers, Ayanthi escorted her sister to the Keenawala railway station to board the train to Polgahawela.

Wilson was proud to observe his four children making their way to the railway station along the banks of the paddy fields.

Wilson, glancing at his wife, Suduhamine, said, "The big girl is like their mother…"

Suduhamine was proud to hear this. But not showing any concern, she responded with fake anger,

"Why only the eldest girl? All four children are like me…"

Wilson as well as wife Suduhamine were a devoted couple and won the hearts of the villagers. Their four children, too, lived with co-operation and love.

Though the four children would go school together, they returned home separately. The two brothers attended daily support classes at Gampaha town after school.

The youngest daughter would return with the eldest sister, except on the days she had to attend training classes for dancing.

Fortunately, Ayanthi had household chores throughout the day to keep her busy.

Ayanthi's daily routine included assisting the mother in preparation of meals, washing siblings' clothes, cleaning rooms and caring for the outdoor plants.

She performed these tasks with much dedication. Sometimes, feigning fake anger on the brothers she would say, "Though you are big now, but still unable to wash your clothes!"

At that, the younger brother would respond, saying,

"OK. OK. But you are the head of the family. Therefore, you must do all this helping…" It would upset Ayanthi.

At that, Ayanthi would glare at the brother, but she secretly adored his statement.

She always presumed that being the eldest female in the family, all daily chores were to be performed by herself.

At times, the mother would scold the younger brother and sister saying,

"Now Sister will do all these. Who will do them after she marries and leaves home?"

At this, both the brother and sister would jokingly respond,

"Where can you find a stilt walking partner to marry her?"

And the reason for this was Ayanthi being well-built in height and size, as compared to her fellow peers.

One day in February 1988, Ayanthi along with the family visited Dunagaha aunt's residence to participate in an Alms giving.

As a habit, she communicated with her relatives and neighbors in the gathering. She had inherited this from her father.

Having passed very well at the G.C.E. Ordinary Level examination in December 1987, she was very relaxed.

After a cordial conversation with the guests, she proceeded to the kitchen of her aunt. On the way she plucked a fruit from a Biling tree, munching some on her way. At that time, she spotted a young boy whom she had not seen earlier.

He was seated on a bench in the dining room.

Having stepped into adolescent age, she experienced an unusual feeling. She could not take her eyes away from him.

She was lost in her thoughts and longed to speak to him. But she had no courage to do so, as he did not look at her. Though she stared him, he did not notice her.

This made her a little angry.

She left that place thinking he was proud but she was determined to speak at least one word with him.

She felt a deep satisfaction observing Sister Kanthi serving tea and refreshments to the guests.

Not thinking twice, she decided to obtain her assistance. Grabbing the refreshment tray from her, she told Kanthi, "You bring the tea!"

She ran towards the proud boy whom she had not had the chance to meet earlier, with the intention of seeing him again.

He was seated at the same place. Her eyes sparkled on seeing him.

She went to him and extended the refreshment tray. "Brother, please help yourself."

Following her, Kanthi said, "Here, I brought the tea too."

But there was no reaction from him.

Ayanthi felt very sad and also angry at him. She decided to tame the proud boy.

She asked, "Brother, from where are you?"

Kanthi responded, "Who?"

Sister Indira, who was close by, said,

"This is Uncle Jaya's son, Sanka," starting the conversation.

Responding, Kanthi remarked, "We were not aware that Uncle Jaya had such an elderly son!" He stared scornfully at all of them.

At that, Sister Indira also inquired,

"Brother, did not you do the Ordinary Level examination this year? What were the results?"

Breaking the silence, he finally replied, "Eight – eight."

Ayanthi, looking at him secretly, replied, "I too got eight – eight."

And Sister Kanthi questioned,

"Were all of them credit passes?"

He replied, "No…one was a distinction."

Ayanthi, responding and looking directly at him, said, "I too got one distinction."

Sister Kanthi probingly asked, "Distinction, for which subject?"

"Buddhism." he replied.

Proud and eyes sparkling, Ayanthi said, "I too got a distinction in Buddhism!"

Looking at her sarcastically, he asked, "What is your height?"

Responding enthusiastically, she said "Five feet and six inches."

He left her, saying resentfully,

"Not certain of your height…bring a ruler to measure same!" This verbal dialog Ayanthi could never forget during her entire lifetime.

Ayanthi's eyes searched for him before she left aunt's house on completion of the alms-giving rituals, but she could not locate him.

With a slight pain she left, and came home. She had a sleepless night, visualizing him.

With a slight smile, she assumed him as a proud fellow.

She decided that a day will come when she will meet him again.

❖

She played badminton with the siblings when an opportunity would arise. Also, caring for flower plants made her life enjoyable.

Watering of betel plants maintained by her father was another task. Ayanthi was proud to overhear father telling mother,

"Betel plants are growing vigorously due to Ayanthi's care!" Mother responded slowly and secretly, looking at Ayanthi, "The day she is gone only we will know the difference!"

Feigning anger, Ayanthi retorted, "Mother, what did you say?"

And Mother responded, glancing at the husband,

"Nothing…"

Father was silent…

Ayanthi relished such moments, she left them thinking, *Heck! She wants to get rid of me…*

Father Wilson in a deep thought, muttered,

"I have a lot of responsibility on the two daughters."

She felt that secretly she was falling in love with him. These thoughts enchanted her.

She smiled to herself.

Her siblings observing her say,

"Looks as if she has fallen in love with a boy," in order to get the attention of the father towards them.

They thought the parents loved the eldest sister more than them, which they despised. This would make Ayanthi upset.

Time flew by…

Ayanthi did not meet that proud boy.

She visited aunt's residence several times with the intention of meeting him. But, fate disappointed her.

She thought he was hiding from her.

She felt abandoned and felt lonely when returning home. She was confused by not being able to meet him.

She tried not to show any such concern to her family.

Meanwhile Ayanthi also attended extra classes at Gampaha town.

She got to meet Wasala during this period. That was through Sister Indira. Though Indira was younger than her, both attended same class.

Ayanthi was thrilled that Wasala was the good-looking friend she was searching for. It did not take much time for her to get acquainted with Wasala as her brother.

Together they ate, drank tea or coffee, and enjoyed.

During intervals they chatted freely, and he revealed that Sanka was his best friend. One day when Wasala was alone, she disclosed on him with a great determination.

She addressed him with doubts of how she is going to ask him the intruding question. "Wasala, can I ask you something?"

Inquisitively looking at her, he replied, "What? You can ask anything."

She questioned, "Why does your friend Sanka not attend this class?"

Looking at the floor, Wasala maintained his silence.

"Why is this? I need to know," Ayanthi insisted. Her insisting voice got his attention.

Wasala replied,

"Due to poor financial status of Sanka, he is unable to come for these classes." He briefly narrated Sanka's life of financial difficulties.

She was shocked by this revelation.

She, however, suppressed her discomfort, and then requested,

"Will you do me a small favor?"

Wasala replied,

"If possible, will do…" Ayanthi ran to her class.

Tearing a page from the notebook, she wrote a small letter. She ran back to Wasala carrying the letter.

She said,

"Wasala, keep this letter inside your book. Do not fail to give this to Sanka." Thrusting the letter to him, she ran back to the class.

She counted the days…until next Saturday.

On that Saturday at the class, she secretly observed Wasala. She felt there was an emptiness in his face.

She could not fathom this situation. She ran to him during the interval. She impatiently asked him, "Where is the reply to my letter?"

"Sanka did not reply..." said Wasala.

At that, she felt all her efforts were destroyed. She repeated,

"Why no reply?"

He said, "I do not know why. But I gave the letter and he read it and put in his pocket."

With a sad face he said, "I did not get a reply from him." She again asked, "Why?"

Wasala replied, "I do not know..."

Insisting, Ayanthi said, "Please tell me...why?"

"How do I know? He read it and put it in his pocket. That is all." Ayanthi, in a subdued voice, asked,

"No reply at all?"

"No..." Wasala replied.

She, in an upset mood, said, "Wait a moment, I will come back soon," and ran back to the classroom.

Again, Ayanthi, tearing a leaf from her notebook, wrote a short letter. She ran back to him without anyone noticing her moments.

Extending the letter to Wasala, she pleaded saying, "Wasala, please give this to Sanka and bring back a reply."

"Will try..." replied Wasala, and placed the letter inside his books.

Returning home, she felt unusual loneliness unlike the other days. She thought that the usual elated feeling was no more. Noticing the same, her mother inquired,

"What happened? Are you not well?"

Replying, she said, "No, nothing at all; having a little headache…as I was attending classes the whole day…" and ran to her bedroom and fell on the bed.

Although she did not have the habit of lying down during the day, she was confused by loneliness and emptiness.

She buried her face in the pillow and was engulfed in her thoughts, which bothered her.

Who is he? Why am I attracted to him? Such thoughts made her uncomfortable.

❖

Next Saturday, she attended the class with much enthusiasm.

She saw Wasala seated in the back row among many other students. She knew she could not meet him until the interval.

She realized that for the past two hours she was not concentrating on what was been taught at the class.

No sooner the interval arrived, she ran to Wasala with many thoughts blurring her mind.

She asked,

"Wasala, did you give the letter to Sanka?"

"Yes, I did."

"Any reply?" she inquired.

His response: "No reply."

It shattered all her valiant efforts.

In an upset mood, she replied, "You are lying."

Wasala responded,

"Why should I? Like the other day, he read and put the letter in his pocket. He did not give me a reply."

She became distraught.

With a drawn face, she went back to her class. On the inside, she was hurting because of the circumstance. She did not know what to do now.

Questioning herself, she asked,

Why am I going after a person whom I do not know and who does not care for me? She was lost in thoughts and felt abandoned.

On and on she felt pain in her heart. In a determined effort she decided, *No! I will write another letter.*

She tore a leaf from the notebook and wrote,

Dear...

She erased and wrote again,

Loving...

She erased that too.

She did not recall how she addressed the previous letter.

Again, addressed him as 'Loving', but could not continue.

Writing her intentions and erasing the same several times. At last, she wrote,

"Loving Sanka,

    I trust you are in good health.

    Why did you not reply to my letter?

    I do not know what to say or write. Can you please send me a reply?

With love, Ayanthi."

She completed the letter.

Interval was over. The classes had commenced by that time. She could not concentrate on what was being taught in the class. Her mind was on the letter and him.

She was despondent.

She spent the remaining two hours with great difficulty. No sooner the class was over, she ran towards Wasala.

She found Sister Indira as an obstacle for her purpose and sought a remedy. She inserted the letter into a book and gave it to Wasala, saying,

"Wasala, here is the book you requested."

Understanding her intentions, he replied, "Okay, okay…" and also said, "I will definitely return the book next week." She retorted, "Now, do not fail this time,"

His response: "Definitely…will bring it back." Which brought her some comfort.

She thought that he understood her situation very well.

It seemed she was lost with her thoughts in the adolescent age. She felt that the enthusiastic feeling she had was slowly leaving her. Younger sister at times complained,

"Sister, what is wrong with you? You have not ironed my uniform properly."

Younger brother, like her younger sister, shouted, "My trousers, too, were not ironed properly."

Sometimes elder brother inquired, "Sister, why have you not cleaned my room today?" As if she had committed a grave offence.

Ayanthi's daily routine of sweeping brothers' room and ironing their clothes used to bring her immense joy.

She felt that joy was no more there now.

Her parents, too, did not find fault with her, though there were short comings, because they were aware that she tended to everybody's need tirelessly.

Sometimes Mother would scold the two brothers and younger sister saying, "Sister Ayanthi does not have special duties to perform. Not a big deal if you all attend to your needs, personally." Which Ayanthi appreciated to hear.

At that time, the radio blurted a song of singer Mrs. Nanda Malani. Ayanthi too, silently joined in.

She counted the days till next Saturday. She at times questioned herself, *Why am I taking trouble to acquaint with this unknown person?* She did not want to think deeply into the matter.

Yet her mind said, *No...no...I definitely must meet this proud boy.*

A smile appeared on her face at the sweet idea of meeting him. On Saturday early morning, she attended the class.

She was much saddened that though she was longing to speak to Wasala who was seated in a back row, she had no opportunity to do so.

She stole a glance at him.

A mild anger arose as she observed that Wasala was absorbed in the lecture.

Unable to control her thoughts, she inquired herself, *Is he not aware that I am expecting a response?*

Unaware of Ayanthi looking at him, he spotted her and signaled her without drawing attention of others. She was overwhelmed by this.

But she had to be patient as the interval was due only in an hour. She felt unable to spend that hour.

When interval arrived, with great enthusiasm she ran towards Wasala, though he was chatting with his friends.

Seeing her walking towards him, he extended the book to her, saying, "Here is the book I borrowed from you."

She grabbed it forcibly. He laughed at that.

Cuddling the book, she was thrilled, and ran into the class.

She took the folded letter from inside the book into her hands with much enthusiasm. She felt elated, and was anxious to know the contents of the letter, which said,

Ayanthi,

Received your letter.

I am fine. Hope you too doing well.

Birds are singing while butterflies are flying...Life is a silent song...

Five fingers are not same in hand (difference between you and me). Hope you will understand what I mean...

Thanking you,
Sanka.

She was sad and anger arose at the very short response.

She was engulfed in a cloud of sorrow and wished to cry out loudly. She glanced around her to check if anybody was observing her.

She felt as though those around her must be laughing at her on the contents of the letter. Anger arose in her, prompting that letter be crushed and thrown off.

Instead, she ran her fingers on the letter. She slowly recited the contents again.

She overheard verses of a love song.

Floating...blue clouds...

She felt devastated...feeling her mind was out of control. That night was a sleepless night for her.

She, in her memory, repeated the contents of his letter.

Though she had not received such a letter from anyone earlier, she experienced many unusual feelings.

She went into solitude. She thought that there is a romantic meaning in the words in the letters of his.

When she finally fell asleep, it was past midnight, as she heard the 12:30 am night-mail train to Vauniya passing Keenawala railway station.

She continued to write letters to Sanka and the messenger was Wasala. She received one reply for three to four letters of hers.

She cherished same. Replies were short.

She felt the replies were loaded with tenderness and love. She felt she was falling in love with him.

But she did not have the courage to convey or write of her love for him. Reciprocating his love, she never received the letter proclaiming his love. She realized this unconditional love for Sanka was generated by herself.

A novel enthusiasm engulfed her as she had not experienced such love except from her two brothers.

But she did not meet him. Sometimes she cried internally.

At that time, she overheard a song from singer Karunarathna Divulgane:

Wind...like you...carried away my heart.

She felt lost thinking of adolescent age and the melodies she heard. She herself inquired as to when or how she could meet him.

Whenever any opportunity would arise, she would visit aunt's residence, hoping she will meet Sanka. But it was not to be so.

Deep sorrow and sadness engulfed her. And she wept…

On several instances, she visualized if she could hide or leave this cruel world. She was tormented by sorrow and loneliness.

At that time, she overheard a song.

You are similar to the wind…which engulfs minds…like trying to steal the flowers…you stole my mind and isolated me and hurt me…finding the sensitive spots. But my mind does not leave you which is a miracle…

She adored this song and thought that song was a part of hers.

She at times wept, hearing this song. But, had no strength to come out of that frame. She had to perform her daily routine house chores as usual.

She was the acting mother on the days her mother fell sick.

Having to attend to the needs of her siblings, she missed school at times. Her parents were very proud of her commitment for this.

❖

In August 1990, she sat for the G.C.E. (Advance Level) examination.

She contemplated if Sanka too will sit for the examination and wished he will pass as they did at the Ordinary Level examination.

On the first day of the exam, she realized that she was ill prepared to sit for the exam, of which she was unconcerned.

She wished they both should get through this exam like the Ordinary Level examination. But she was not fortunate to qualify to enter the university.

She was depressed on hearing that Sanka too did not qualify. She had no way of sharing either the information or the disappointment.

Attending extra classes were no more as the G.C.E. (A/L) examination was over.

She realized that the only opportunity to get information on Sanka was also obstructed now.

Due to this, having got to know that Wasala was attending an English class, she too joined the same, with the intention of contacting Sanka through Wasala.

Time flew by…

Ayanthi received information that Sanka has secured employment to stabilize his finances. This message brought her sorrowful feelings as he also was in the same age group as her, but he had to take care of the wellbeing of his family in that young age.

She was devastated as she did not receive letters from him anymore.

One day, Ayanthi's attention was directed towards a high-pitched conversation taking place among her parents.

Walking towards them, she inquired, "What is this all about?"

Her parents saw her coming towards them and abandoned the conversation. She implored,

"Are you having an argument?"

Mother seated sorting vegetables, ignored her.

Sitting beside Mother, she assisted her in sorting the vegetables. Father leaving them alone, departed when mother said,

"I do not know how to say this," and became silent. Ayanthi inquired,

"What is it?"

Mother looked at her and Ayanthi observed that her eyes were in tears. Ayanthi pleaded,

"Mother, what is the problem? What happened? Tell me now."

"Nothing."

At which she said, "If nothing, why are you crying now?"

She was confused as she had not come across her parents quarreling and also for resolving the curiosity in her mind Ayanthi pleaded her mother, "Please tell me, what is it?" Mother, sadly looking at her, said, "Father said there is a marriage proposal for you." It stunned her, unable to believe same.

Ayanthi forcibly asked, "Proposal for me? What for?" With the intention of solving the issue.

Mother, gathering the sorted vegetables, said, "You better ask from your father." And kept the sorted vegetables on the fireplace. In a firm tone, Ayanthi responded,

"Okay. I will ask from Father." She left mother with great sorrow.

But she knew she had no courage to ask him directly, as she had never questioned Father's authority in the past.

Though she fully understood about the proposal, she never expected in her wildest dreams that it will come so soon.

Instantly, she felt immense sorrow and felt she could cry loudly. She ran to her room, closing the door behind her.

Leaning her back on the closed door, she closed her eyes for a while. She felt devastated at the word 'proposal'.

Falling on her bed, she buried her face in the pillow.

She felt like crying, feeling her mind was paralyzed and as if a load was on top of her head.

Unknowingly, her eyes were in tears. She felt the whole world had collapsed.

She fell asleep and felt same, waking up only when her younger sister returned home after extra classes – who was sat on her bed.

Younger sister, stroking Ayanthi's head, asked, "Sister, when is the groom expected?"

Waking up and startled, Ayanthi inquired, "Groom? What groom?"

She got down from the bed, tying her loose hair.

Sister observed that Ayanthi's eyes were reddish and swollen which she did not probe about. She left Ayanthi's bed room realizing that Ayanthi was in an angry mood.

That night at the dinner table there was not much discussion unlike other days.

Father Wilson, as a habit, sat with the four children only for dinner. Despite requests from all, mother tending to all their needs, did not sit with them for dinner.

Breaking the silence, Father said, "Ayanthi, a proposal was received for you from Kurunagala," while looking directly at her. No one spoke.

Father continued, "This is a good proposal, the party is wealthy."

Ayanthi secretly observed that her brothers and sister were not enjoying their dinner. She felt crying out loudly, and felt that the food she swallowed was stuck in her throat.

"Have you finished eating?" Mother asked the youngest son.

Unlike the other days when he spent more time at dinner, today he rose and left early from the table.

The elder brother, assuming that he is mature enough, asked, "Why is this sudden proposal for Ayanthi?"

Father replied, "Son, a girl must get married when she is mature."

In anger, younger sister asked, "Has the elder sister reached marrying age?"

Silencing all, the father replied, "Now, what is her age? She has also completed attending school…" Pushing the chair forcibly with anger, younger sister left the dinner table. But, tone of Father's voice was firm.

Ayanthi did not remember if she had her dinner, though her plate was in front of her. She felt as if a heavy load had fallen on top of her head.

Her throat was parched.

In her own mind, she asked, *now what is happening here?*

As Ayanthi was walking with the plate in hand towards the kitchen, she heard Father saying,

"Very soon the Groom's party will visit us here…" That was a sleepless night for Ayanthi.

Long after she laid down on the bed, she heard her sister calling her again. Younger sister repeated, "Sister?"

It did not take long for Ayanthi to soak the pillow with tears she had buried her face in. Younger sister inquired,

"Sister, what is happening here? Why is the father in search of a partner for you at this time?"

Sleep also eluded younger sister today though on other days she instantly fell asleep falling on the bed. Ayanthi maintained silence; not replying…buried her face further in the pillow. She felt a heavy load on top of her head. She was unable to fathom anything as no thoughts came to her mind.

That was an ominous night and midnight passing with an owl breaking the silence intermittently.

Many thoughts clouded her mind that deserted night.

She was not in control of her mind. She felt that her thoughts were not functioning and were dead.

Next morning, with a sad face Ayanthi asked mother, "Why are you searching for a partner for me so early?"

Observing the unusual depleted splendor on her daughter's face, Mother felt sad and said with a view of satisfying Ayanthi,

"Daughter, what can I do? I too knew about it only when your father told me. Anyway, a girl has to leave the parents when she marries."

In a firm tone, Ayanthi retorted,

"I do not require a partner now!"

At that moment, Ayanthi did not notice Father entering the kitchen when he said, "We are not meaning harm to you by this proposal."

Ayanthi did not disagree as she had never done so.

She always had highest regard, love, affection and obedience for the father. Father continued to say,

"The boy is from Kurunagala's respectable wealthy family, and he is rich."

Ayanthi left the kitchen, ignoring Father's comments. As if in a dream, she heard him say, "The family will soon be visiting us here."

She was paralyzed and felt that her dress was soaked with sweat, thinking, *what is happening here? God, what I am to do now*? She ran to her room.

On reaching her room, she fell on the bed burying face in the pillow, as she could not do anything else.

She cried until her eyes were swollen and red.

She had lost control of all household's chores she performed earlier. She was not in a mood to tend to them.

Overhearing *Tied by a golden thread*, a song of vocalist Mrs. Nanda Malani confused her some more.

God, what am I to do? she repeatedly asked herself. Her mind in a frenzy. Unable to control her youthful mind she decided, *I will ask Sanka*, and firmly wished to do so. *But why do I have to ask him? What relationship do I have with him? Does he love me? Truly, does he love me? What will he do… What will he say?*

Her mind was quizzing her with a whole lot of matters… Nothing was clear.

She listened to the song of singer Mrs. Nanda Malini, *When whole world is lost, disappointing and burning, a loving word from you will cure my soul.*

I will speak to Sanka…and tell him everything. But will he believe me? Does he really love me?

Such thoughts clouded her mind, with nobody in sight, and being unobserved, she wrote him a letter:

Dear Sanka,

Trust you are in good health.

I need to meet you very soon. Very urgent please.

On Sunday after the class, I will be going with Sister Kanthi to Aunt's Dunagaha residence. Please come to Gampaha town bus stand by 11:00 am without fail, to meet me.

Yours Lovingly, Ayanthi.

"Ayanthi, there…Sanka has arrived."

Eyes of Ayanthi glowed at hearing this, and pretending to be surprised, said, "Where, Sister? I do not see him yet."

Kanthi replied, "There he is!"

Ayanthi asked, "Where? I do not see him."

Kanthi with a loud laughter grabbed Ayanthi by her shoulders, showing the direction Sanka was, saying,

"There is your boyfriend."

Ayanthi feigned irritability, and angrily said, "Just do not play the fool."

Then, she saw him.

Instantly, her face turned white.

Kanthi observing that Ayanthi's face had become as a defoliated flower shook Ayanthi's shoulders saying,

"What happened? What is bothering you?"

Kanthi had analyzed the situation clearly and to pacify Ayanthi, said, "You should smile when you meet your boyfriend!"

Kanthi walked towards Sanka and to break the silence asked,

"Brother, did you arrive early?" In order to start a conversation. Sanka turned his face to the ground and replied,

"Yes…a little while ago…"

He and Ayanthi were speechless and dumb. Only Kanthi spoke and asked Ayanthi, "Shall we go in that bus today? We also have to come back." Saying this, she started to walk towards the bus leaving to Dunagaha town.

Following Kanthi, Ayanthi and Sanka walked together to the bus.

In the bus, Kanthi arranged to seat Ayanthi and Sanka on the same seat and made her way to a seat at the rear with a little smile on her face.

This was a novel experience for both Ayanthi and Sanka.

In her earlier life, except with her two brothers, she had not sat with another boy on the same seat.

She continued to stare out of the window…Sanka too was speechless.

She felt her heartbeat going up rapidly, and her mouth ran dry.

Thinking as to why Sanka was not speaking, unobserved, she stole a glance at him. But he was only looking ahead.

Though she felt like grabbing his hand, she was frightened to do so. *Will he scold me?*

Will others observe us? Such thoughts baffled her.

With a mighty effort, she controlled her thoughts.

She pondered, *From where shall I start?* At that moment, bus started the journey.

Passing the Bo tree of Gampaha town, he queried, "Why did you ask me to come?"

At that she felt her mouth ran dry; she was unable to speak. She felt that she was about to burst into tears.

However, she somehow controlled herself, and for a while, closed her eyes. With firm determination she decided, *Yes, I will tell him everything.*

He repeated, "Why did you request me to come?"

At that moment, the bus passed Asgiriya junction. She replied, "What did you say?" While not looking directly at him.

Not looking at her, he repeated, "What is the issue?"

It stirred a sharp anger in Ayanthi.

With a mighty effort she controlled herself. With a firm and definite tone, she asked,

"Why did you not send a direct reply to my letters?" She observed him sighing with a 'hmm'.

She told him, "Please speak up."

Half-heartedly he looked at her and breaking the silence said, "At this moment, I am unable to say anything on this matter." Her face displayed anxiety and in an irritated voice she asked, "Why is that?"

At that moment, she observed him looking at her indirectly. With a depressed, tone he replied,

"You very well know my situation."

With anger rising, she asked him,

"Why can you not give me a direct answer?"

Replying, he said, "You very well know I have two sisters to be looked after…and of course, your family is rich…"

Unable to control her anger, she retorted, "Enough…enough! Are you waiting till I am given away in marriage to somebody else?" Looking straight at her, he replied,

"That will not happen."

With tears about to burst, she replied, "Why not? It will happen that way…"

She disliked seeing him staring in front, unable to communicate. She made a firm determination to inform Sanka of everything. Wiping tears with a handkerchief, she said,

"A partner is visiting to see me for marriage." His eyes popping out, he asked,

"What?"

She, in a depressed tone mixed with feeble and sorrow feelings, repeated, "Yes, a groom will visit to see me very soon."

She felt him releasing a long sigh but had no courage to look at him. She heard as it in a dream, Sister Kanthi from behind saying, "Ayanthi, the bus stop is near for us to get down." Although they had travelled in the bus for around 40 minutes, their conversation was limited, of which she was sad.

Looking straight at him, she asked, "What am I to do now?"

She felt that he was trying to avoid her gaze.

In a sad tone, she asked him, "Why are you doing this to me?" He did not reply.

Maintaining silence, they got down from the bus.

Great sorrow prevailed in Ayanthi's mind and wished she should cry out loud. But there was no place for that now.

Hiding her sorrow, and in order to convince Kanthi that she was happy now, she told him,

"Thank you for accepting my invitation to meet."

Kanthi, speaking to Sanka, informed,

"Brother, we are taking leave of you now." It brought great sorrow and pain to Ayanthi.

Avoiding their looks, he left them, muttering, "hmm…"

Both of them, who had never been in love, did not anticipate that this will be their first and last meeting.

Ayanthi did not in her wildest dreams imagine that this love will be over even before it started.

In an instant, she decided to terminate the unspoken playful and fond dream of love for him.

Residence of businessman Wilson was a hub of activity. The aroma of sweetmeats being prepared drifted to other houses in the vicinity.

Very often, women from the neighborhood were visitors to Wilson's house.

Wilson as well as family members were a loyal family to all villagers. Due to this, his residence was always patronized by visitors.

Some visitors secretly whispered,

"A groom is visiting to meet Wilson's eldest daughter." Another said,

"She is a very lucky girl."

In the midst of them, Ayanthi felt that all was lost and her life was shattered. At times she felt anger towards Sanka.

With great pain, she questioned herself, *Why did Sanka ignore me? After all the efforts I made?*

At times she did a self-analysis of him. *Do I really love Sanka?*

Truly, do I love him? No...no...

It cannot be...

I have never told him so...Have I written to him so? No...no... I have not written...

So...how will I know if Sanka does really love me? I am not able to expect his love under these circumstances!

Such thoughts weighed heavily on her head.

Great sorrow and pain surrounded her mind. She felt lonely and desolated.

Her sister arrived with a query, "Sister, are you going to wear the blue saree?" It woke her from the dream world.

Ayanthi replied, "I am not wearing any saree." Glaring at her sister, she said, "I do not want to get married yet."

Sister addressing and holding Ayanthi's hand tightly, said, "Everything is arranged now..." In order to pacify her.

Ayanthi about to burst into tears replied, "Why cannot anybody understand my plight?" Sister holding Ayanthi's hand tightly said, "Can I ask you something?"

With a questionable look on her face, Ayanthi asked, "What?"

Sister looking straight at Ayanthi's face queried, "Do you have a boyfriend?"

Hearing this, Ayanthi was stunned!

Looking at her sister, she was speechless for a moment. She had not left any room for anybody to know of her unspoken love story.

Ayanthi in an angry voice said, "I do not have any boyfriend."

Sister replied, "Are you sure? If you do have someone, we can speak to the father."

Ayanthi burying her face in the pillow said, "Please leave me alone, and go away from here."

Younger sister understood Ayanthi's need to be alone, so she left the bedroom. That night too was a sleepless night.

She felt that this particular night will be an extended one. She overheard vocalist Mr. Amaradewa's song,

When the sun goes down in the evening...

The pillow her head was resting was soaked with tears. She visualized the evening she bid him farewell.

She felt her mind and body were paralyzed, and the morning arriving with no hope at all. She wished she could cry out loudly.

❖

Since morning, her house was a hive of activity.

Ayanthi did least anticipate that particular day will change her life and destiny.

Though with reluctance, she woke up early to assist her mother and aunt in the kitchen, Ayanthi could not think beyond, and felt that there was no end in sight.

A day of activity had dawned for businessman Wilson. Arrangements were crowding his mind.

At times he found his way to the kitchen inquiring from his wife, "Suduhamine, are there any short comings?"

He was immaculately dressed in a white sarong and a short sleeved white shirt. At that time, the aunt informed

37

Ayanthi, "You need not be present in the kitchen, please go and get ready." Ayanthi woke up from her dreams.

Sister Kanthi taking Ayanthi's hand headed her to her room saying, "Let us go from here."

Kanthi's presence was a source of consolation to Ayanthi. Ayanthi gripping Kanthi's hand asked, "What am I to do now?"

Kanthi replied, "We will face it as it comes."

While rubbing Ayanthi's head in order to pacify her, she continued further saying,

"I know that Sanka may love you, but due to his present situation, he may be unable to make any decision now." Ayanthi's eyes were overflowing with tears and a firm cry erupted in her.

Kanthi rubbing Ayanthi's head to calm her said, "Do not cry now. We will face the situation as it comes."

"Just because a bridegroom visits you, it is not mandatory to marry him." Expecting Ayanthi to get some consolation.

Ayanthi heard her younger brother screaming, "Father, a car is approaching, seems to be the bridegroom's party!"

Ayanthi felt her heartbeat increasing and murmured, "God, What am I to do now?"

At that moment, her aunt and mother approached and said, "Ayanthi, come here."

Ayanthi was taken aback.

She felt that her mother, concealing her grief, had come to accompany her to meet the bridegroom.

The blue saree purchased for her lay on her bed.

Ayanthi was dressed in a long black skirt and a white sleeved blouse.

Nobody objected when she refused to wear the saree, in order to face the bridegroom. For a moment Ayanthi closed her eyes and took a firm hold of her mind.

Led by the mother, she also firmly held the aunt's hand and came out of her bedroom. Through the seated visitors, she walked towards the bridegroom.

Unintentionally she kept her hands together and welcomed him. Looking secretly at him, she noticed that he was shorter than her. She was dumb founded.

On her aunt's persistence, she sat next to him. She felt running away from there.

But controlling her emotions she restrained, as such action will cause disrespect to her father's reputation.

As a custom, her father with a glass of water in hand invited all for tea saying, "Shall we have tea and discuss other matters?"

To the bridegroom, he said, "Son, help yourself to another piece of milk rice."

Though seated next to him, Ayanthi did not eat or drink anything, as she was not in a mood to do so.

She felt her whole body trembling and thought of running away from there. He looked at her and queried,

"Are you sitting for the G.C.E. Advance Level examination again?" Breaking the silence, she replied,

"No."

Confirming same, he replied, "Yes...now it is not necessary."

His father joining their conversation said, "Yes of course, now she will have to learn how to run our present business."

Unobserved, Ayanthi glanced at her father, and noticed his eyes were glowing with satisfaction.

Although she thought again of running away from there, she forcibly refrained herself as her father's reputation would be affected.

Where is the love…I sought from you…

That verse from a song kindled her mind and she wailed thinking, *Sanka, where are you?*

As if in a dream, she overheard bridegroom's father saying, "We will take your leave now."

"Why postpone this marriage?"

"Will let you know of an early date."

By that time, Ayanthi was in her room having to take off her dress. She felt that her whole world had collapsed.

Burying her face in the pillow, she started to cry. That night was a prolonged one for her.

She had to consider many things.

Though all at home did not speak to each other, they thought that their father was happy of the visit of the bridegroom and his family.

It was past midnight, and she thought her environment was desolate.

*Night without sleep…*that verse from the song encouraged her to seek solace. Advancing towards her writing table, she sat and commenced writing a long letter.

Dear Sanka,

Why cannot you understand my plight? A bridegroom visited here today to see me. I cannot understand your silence.

Are you unable to fathom my situation? I do not know if I am bothering you.

But you are my whole world. Why do not you appreciate that? Hope to hear from you soon.

Yours Lovingly, Ayanthi.

Time flew from days to weeks. Sanka replied to the letter.

Dear Ayanthi,

I do not think you are in good spirits, but I am helpless.

I regret my inability to send you a letter for your satisfaction.

As intimated earlier, I am not in a position to make a decision myself alone.

You are well aware, that I have two younger sisters to take care of. I am loaded with responsibilities, as the only brother of my sisters.

Also, your father will never permit an affair of this nature.

Further, if he comes to know of this affair, that will definitely destroy our family relationship.

Due to this you will have to bear with me, for a little more time. Yours lovingly,

Sanka.

It reminded Ayanthi of a verse in a song,
The day when the sun goes down.
She had read the letter in one breath and did not have a clear mind to understand his position.

She grieved and cried continuously.

A sharp anger filling her mind, and she queried herself, *Sanka…why are you doing this to me?*

Burying her face in the pillow, she cried without a break.

One day, the bridegroom Aruna, came in search of her to the extra class she attended in Gampaha.

Spotting her coming out of the class, he got down from the car and approached her.

He said, "Ayanthi, I visited your residence, and they informed me that you were attending this class. Come, I will drop you home."

He opened the door of the vehicle for her to enter. She was dumb founded and was scared to reply.

Other than submitting to his request, she had no courage to decline his offer. She thought she was trapped.

Grieving in her thoughts she queried, *God…what can I do now?*

While seated in the car and maintaining total silence up to her residence, she accompanied him.

She gave short replies to the questions he asked, as she had no courage to show any dislike, as she had to maintain her father's dignity.

That day, she wrote the decisive letter to Sanka.

Dear Sanka,

I require a straight reply from you.

Do you like me? Or dislike me?

Today, the bridegroom visited me after the class. This may be the final letter from me.

Do not hurt me anymore!

She never received a reply from Sanka for that final letter of hers.

❖

Days turned into weeks and months, and flew by. Ayanthi listening to the lyrics of the song,

*Love entwined by fingers tied by a gold cord…is it yours or mine? Tomorrow I will bid farewell to you…*broke down in tears.

Businessman Wilson's residence was turning out to be a grand wedding venue. Daily, the house was filled with relatives, well-wishers and neighbors.

Ayanthi had made up her mind to depart from her village with an unknown stranger, as she had to uphold the dignity of her father.

She had to oblige by her father's aspirations.

Further, as she was the eldest daughter, she had to protect the future welfare of her siblings.

Reluctantly, she sent a wedding invitation to Sanka.

Amid the beating of drums, she was seated on the wedding stage with a made-up smile and greeted the guests.

But nobody could wipe out the hollow feeling inside her mind. At that instant her eyes met him.

He has come…

Sanka has come to bid farewell to me, she thought. She felt running to him and embracing him.

With a mighty effort, she controlled such emotions.

She made her way towards the window and saw him looking at her, reminding her of the song…

Tied by a gold cord…

Both were dumbstruck. They were unable to communicate. She broke the silence by inquiring,

"Sanka, you arrived only now?"

Unable to respond, he was silent, staring at the ground. She could not bear his silence.

Looking at you…I wail…unable to pluck…and dreaming of mountain Hanthane… These lyrics of the song, she felt, was echoing in her ears…

Looking at the ground, he said, "I have become desolate! Anyway, all the best to you."

A long sigh escaped from her.

She felt that her heart has stopped beating and was unable to fathom how she can depart from him forever.

But now definitely, she had to leave him.

With a great effort, she concealed her grief and fond memories of him.

She got into the wedding car leaving her relatives, close friends, neighbors and above all, Sanka, who was her life…

She felt that this chapter of her life was closed forever and terminated the first journey in her life.

02

She used to remember Sanka at times, when she was pampering her baby. A memento given as a gift from Sanka was lying on the dressing table.

Though physically not present on many occasions, she felt his presence in her mind.

She remembered going to school along the paddy fields, as well as enjoying her trips in the train with her friends.

Writing secret letters to Sanka brought her sweet memories. But at times she was distressed and engulfed in sorrow thinking of the enjoyable life spent earlier and she felt that she was a prisoner now.

In the massive and luxurious house, she felt lonely and full of emptiness. But suppressing all these feelings, she continued to face the challenges of her present life.

She devotedly attended to the daily household commitments; apart from attending to the needs of the husband, child and husband's parents, she also took care of their welfare.

She felt she was a well accomplished woman now. Her son took away all her fancy dreams.

Kissing his cheeks, she sighed sometimes, not realizing why she did it.

At times she assisted the husband in his business.

Though it was not pleasant, she felt that was her obligation.

❖

Time flew by…

One day, on an invitation received, she attended along with her husband and child a wedding of an aunt of the husband.

Again, she spotted him…whom she had not seen for more than a year after her wedding day.

Surprised, she thought, *Sanka has come here?* She was astounded.

Dumbfounded, she regretted unable to fathom what to do now. On recognizing them, Sanka made his way towards them.

Ayanthi introduced Sanka to her husband, Aruna, as an old schoolmate. His face did not show any change.

Sanka, collecting the infant child, held him close to his chest cuddling him. She was devastated, feeling she could cry out loudly.

However, she controlled her emotions.

Observing Sanka cuddling her child, she felt that though he was happy and smiling, there was a trace of sadness on his face.

She thought he was not exposing such feelings and contemplated if she had caused any injustice to him.

She wept, thinking how did he accept and bear all this? Returning home, sleep totally evaded her that night.

Wailing in her mind, *Why was I unable to make you mine?* she thought, with pain in her heart.

❖

Only three days remained for celebrations of the first birthday of the child. Husband Aruna's ambition was to hold birthday celebrations at a grand scale.

He inquired, "What more are the shortcomings?"

Ayanthi replied, "Nothing."

"What is already there is sufficient."

"We will celebrate this at a small scale."

"Further, try to understand that son will not understand about all this."

But Aruna disagreed. He said,

"I have to go to town and will be back soon." He departed after kissing his playful son's face.

Nobody ever imagined at that moment Aruna's kissing of his son and seeing Ayanthi will be the final occasion.

Two hours after Aruna's departure from the residence, Ayanthi spotted a friend of his having a heated discussion with the parents of Aruna.

At that moment parents started wailing loudly.

Unable to understand the reason, Ayanthi quickly made her way towards the parents, and inquired,

"Father…Mother…what has happened?" Mother wailing said,

"Oh, my beloved son is no more!"

Dazed, she could not recall if she heard what the father told her soon after.

She firmly cuddled her son and realized that she had no tears at all to flow out from her eyes.

As if in her dreams, she overheard somebody asking, "How did he die?"

Someone replied,

"His car met with an accident!"

She was not in a mood to speak to anyone, and soon after, vaguely remembered visit of her parents, brothers and sister.

Embracing them, she cried.

She noticed her father with eyes tearing, trying to avoid her eyes. She felt that he was blaming himself for the injustice done to her.

Amidst sorrowful relatives, friends and neighbors, Aruna was ready to depart from this world.

She thought, due to an ill fate, his death coincided on the first birthday of their son. She bid farewell to his body, cuddling the child.

Though it was a very short period, she reminisced the time spent with Aruna was very peaceful.

Ayanthi's eyes were filled with tears. She had no strength to weep loudly.

If she did, nobody noticed her.

As if in a dream, she spotted Sanka shouldering Aruna's coffin and walking towards the cemetery. With a confused mind, miserable thoughts invaded her. But she had no courage to be certain or think that he was Sanka.

When night passed by, visitors one by one started leaving the funeral house.

Ayanthi, carrying the son, bid farewell to all who were leaving. She did so, only because of her obligations and not with any feeling.

Spotting Sanka seated alone, she went towards him cuddling the child. Breaking silence she queried,

"Sanka, when did you arrive here?"

No sooner the child saw him, he jumped onto his arms. Maintaining dead silence, he began playfully cuddling the child.

For Ayanthi, that was unbearable and wished she could cry out loudly. But she took control of such emotions.

She inquired, "Why do not you speak? Is it because this place is uncommon to you?"

But he did not glance her way.

She thought that his face was full of sorrow and repentance.

Her days passed by without any special expectations. But she was firm on her belief to bring up the child well.

She was definite on her belief that she will do her utmost to bring up her child well as his mother.

Relentlessly, she attended to her husband's alms giving arrangements.

Parents of Aruna gave their undivided love and protection for her and the infant grandchild. All their requirements were fulfilled to maximum with no shortcomings.

In the absence of Aruna, she was disinclined to visit her parents and only visited them occasionally.

Her only ambition was to bring up the son well, to make him a useful citizen to the society.

Days turned to weeks, months, and years passed by.

Despite her parents as well as Aruna's parent requested to find a suitable partner for the future, it was totally ignored by her.

With a firm determination, she always informed them that her ferment ambition was to bring up her child well with her own efforts.

Ayanthi's father had a nagging notion, that he had committed a great injustice to her. But Ayanthi did not accept that, and pacified her father saying,

"Father, you did this for my benefit, but this is my fate." While silencing anybody present.

Regularly, her father, including younger brother, visited her residence and looked into the welfare of her and child, which brought her immense relief.

Her elder brother who was associated in her father's business, occasionally visited. But did not stay for a long time.

Despite this she felt visits were a tower of strength for her. Ayanthi's sister frequently telephoned to inquire of their wellbeing.

She felt that her mother will be weeping silently and telephoned her saying, "Mother, what can we do? This must be the destiny of mine." It further multiplied mother's sorrow and agony. Mother, responding angrily and forcibly, blamed the father, saying,

"That was due to your father's ambition to give you in marriage to a wealthy family." At that moment, grieving, Ayanthi felt helpless and was forced to maintain silence.

At times, Ayanthi pondered, *where is Sanka now? What is he doing now? Does he still remember me?* But then would instantly change her thoughts, thinking, *why should I think of him? It is a sin. Further, I was married and now a widow. Therefore, why should I again think of him?*

Her thoughts were in a turbulence, and she felt pain inside her.

Unable to fall asleep at night and during the day, thoughts of Sanka came to her mind but she instantly dismissed them, only with the intention of not causing any ill respect to Sanka.

One day in the evening, Ayanthi in a relaxed state was enjoying a cup of tea. Her child was playing in the garden alone.

Parents of Aruna too were seated nearby. But Ayanthi did not take notice of them. Breaking the silence, Aruna's father said,

"Ayanthi."

Her face instantly flushed with anxiety. Ayanthi now focused her attention on them. Father-in-law continuing said,

"Is it ok by you if we ask you something?"

With anxiety developing, Ayanthi contemplated what were they going to inquire her.

From the corner of her eye, she saw Aruna's mother staring at the ground. Leaving no room for Ayanthi to think further, Father-in-law said,

"If you like, we will propose our eldest son Jayarathne to you."

Shocked, she could barely retain the cup of tea she was holding in her hand. She became helpless, and felt her breathing increasing.

Continuing further, Father-in-law said,

"We do not want to force you, but you know his wife too passed away almost a year ago. Furthermore, your son is young and needs the care of a father."

Ayanthi hearing this, felt she was only dreaming. She felt as though a big rock had fallen on top of her head.

Aruna's elder brother, Jayarathne, was fifteen years older than her. And she knew very well that he was the boisterous member of their family. That was a sleepless night for her.

As in a dream, she heard the lyrics of the song,

On this sleepless night…why cry hiding behind this mist of tears…of the first love…

Ayanthi had no alternative, but to consent to marry Jayarathne on the insistence of the parents of hers as well as Aruna's, in order to shoulder future responsibilities.

Though she had no expectations, she could not bear to see her parents in anguish. She also had to consider in deep the future wellbeing of her son.

Ayanthi felt that she had passed the second journey of her life with two years of married life, as well as another two as a widow along with her son.

<h1 style="text-align:center">03</h1>

She married Jayarathne.

Being mother to her son, she was also stepmother to Jayarathne's son.

She was well aware of Jayarathne's boisterous habits as well as his strict regulations. Also, that his wife, Surangi, who succumbed to cancer, did not receive his love and affection during their married life.

This was due to Ayanthi performing bulk of the duties for that family. Before Surangi's demise, Ayanthi's association with Surangi was like sisters. They did not consider it, as young and old basis.

On a background of this nature, Ayanthi was not obliged to marry Jayarathne.

However, she had to give due consideration to her future and take a firm decision as well as satisfy her parent's aspirations.

Jayarathne was a reputed businessman of the area. His firm and decisive principles of business were well known. His parents were well aware of them and did not interfere on his decisions.

Jayarathne's sole intention was to become the best businessman of his area. In order to achieve this goal easily, he used to lend money on interest. Soon he became a wealthy person in a short period.

Visitors to the marriage of Ayanthi to Jayarathne was restricted to the two families on a decision made by Jayarathne. No outsiders were invited.

Further, Ayanthi had to depart from the residence of Jayarathne's parents to live in the residence of Jayarathne.

Sorrow engulfed Ayanthi, on leaving the comfortable residence of ex-husband Aruna. Though it was a brief period, she felt it was a memorable lifetime experience.

She departed with a load of expectations of being a mother to two sons and to spend her life with her new sole partner.

She pondered this to be the starting point of the third chapter of her life's journey.

Furthermore, even in her wildest dreams she did not anticipate that this period is the beginning of a fateful era.

She toiled daily with great effort for two children's welfare. She carried out all these tasks with a lot of commitment and enthusiasm.

In return, she received only pain from present husband, Jayarathne.

Sometimes he used to smash the cooking utensils on the floor, screaming the food was not palatable. In a rage at times, he smashed the plates and mugs on the floor.

He used to beat her, holding her hair and smashed her head against the wall, frequently. He returned home under the influence of liquor or was drunk when at home.

With cash flowing in abundance, he also had many friends, for association.

Intoxicated by drinking along with his friends, he would return home to quarrel with her, which Ayanthi was well aware of and kept dead silence on her part.

Considering her silence as a threat for no reason, he berated not only her, but also all her family members.

This she could hardly bear. Also realizing that the two children were frightened, she cuddled and pacified them.

At that time, he would beat not only her, but also the children. She bore all this intimidation without any complaint.

On one instance, due to his beatings, her hearing developed a weakness. Beating she received on her face split her lips, and also loss of vision in one eye. Beating on her hips caused immense damage to her skeleton.

In her wildest dreams, she never anticipated that her life will become miserable so soon.

Sometimes, memories of Sanka enveloped her. Memento received from him was lying on her dressing table. But her mind refused to accept such thoughts for a long time, and tears flowed relentlessly from her eyes.

Now she was the servant of the house. Waking up early morning at 4 o' clock, she would go back to sleep past mid night.

Apart from not having sound sleep, she could not enjoy her meals.

But she continued to nourish the two children and looked after their welfare. She was totally committed in carrying out her duties as their mother.

In the absence of love and affection from the father, she fulfilled them abundantly. Tirelessly, she carried out these tasks.

She did not receive any appreciation, a single day from her husband.

Passing midnight and totally intoxicated husband's arrival, she could not have her dinner.

On one occasion, she had to assist her struggling husband to come out of the vehicle.

At times, she was humiliated by his friends who supported intoxicated husband into the house.

Daily, she had to massage his legs until he fell asleep, failing to do would result in physical beating.

Jayarathne was so brutal that at times he used to beat her with any object within his reach, apart from using his hands and legs.

All this was well known by parents of Jayarathne as well as Ayanthi's.

Though she did not utter a word about these assaults, all of them knew what she was going through and she was helpless.

Sometimes the two sons shared what they saw and shared of these assaults with grandparents. But nobody dared to interfere on these matters.

Cursing, at times she thought why her life was become so cruel.

Only solace she got was from her younger brother, who visited her to inquire about her wellbeing.

Her parents as well as elder brother and sister curtailed their visits, due to Jayarathne's assaults on Ayanthi, as well as his dislike of their visits.

Though younger brother visited, analyzing the situation, he would not stay long. Ayanthi could not bear this at all. But she was helpless in this regard.

The two children adored their younger uncle who brought them sweets of their preference to satisfy them.

Jayarathne was bit controlled only to his mother's sister who had worked as a teacher and had taken care of him in his childhood. Ayanthi got some consolation during her visits and on counseling he received from her.

One day, her younger brother informed that Sanka is to marry soon.

Hearing this, she felt unbearable sorrow and that she could cry out loudly. She could not understand if that was due to the love she felt for him or to get rid of the sorrow inside her.

She let out a long sigh, thinking, if Sanka was with me, my life will not be like this. Thinking of him, she indulged in self-analyzing and considered that the decision Sanka took was appropriate, of not marrying her.

Time flew by. She was in great pain due to restricted visits by her parents and siblings.

Demise of her parents as well as well-loved in-laws brought her great distress. She felt that she was lonely in this world, as nobody was present to share her sorrows and joy.

She was restricted to a specified area, and was not permitted to step out of the house. That was due to Jayarathne's dislike of her associating and communicating with anybody.

By supplying all household needs, her visits to the market were also blocked.

Due to demise of both parents-in-law, unlike earlier, she also had to assist Jayarathne in his business matters. But handling of cash in the business was prohibited for her.

Even for an essential need, if ever she required money, she had to beg immensely from him.

Day by day, her life was becoming hell. Almost every day, she received bad news.

One day, Jayarathne came home at an unusual time, causing anxiety in her, he said, "Get ready to visit your father's residence."

She inquired, "Why suddenly?"

He firmly replied, "No need of any talk. I told you to get ready!"

Well aware of his arrogance, not responding, she got ready along with the two children.

With great anxiety, she along with the two children got into the vehicle. She felt a heavy load on her head.

Even during the journey, the conversation was limited. He did not specify why this visit was so sudden.

But when he said,

"Your younger brother was admitted to hospital." She felt her heartbeat increasing. He did not reply when she inquired, "What happened to him?"

She could not fathom this news and silently wept. She wondered if this was the way of life's journey for everyone.

As the vehicle turned into her parent's house, she observed a large gathering in the garden. She was dumbstruck, unable to fathom anything. She was unable to understand what was happening there.

Her younger sister came running towards the vehicle as she got down and said, "Sister, your younger brother has departed from us." While crying out loudly.

Ayanthi felt the whole world had collapsed. Hot tears filled her eyes. Unable to fathom any of this, she cried and wept. Nobody was present to share her sorrow.

Death of her younger brother, whom she dearly loved, made her totally miserable now.

Embracing the stable body of the brother in the coffin, she wept. She thought that an irreplaceable void has descended in her life with the death of the brother.

Her younger brother had passed away due to a heart failure which he had experienced while performing his duties at the site. Home was fully crowded with his staff, relatives, friends and villagers.

On that silent evening, after brother's cremation, she again spotted him. Sanka had arrived.

For a moment, she needed to act dumb as Sanka was trying to avoid her piercing looks. But unlimited attachments made her to walk towards him and she inquired,

"Sanka, what time did you arrive?"

In response, Wasala who was always present as a friend of Sanka replied, "We arrived in the evening."

But Sanka, avoiding her eyes, stared at the ground continuously. She deplored Sanka's silence.

Wasala informed that they had also visited the cemetery for her brother, Ruwan's, last rites.

Instantly, Ayanthi recalled that Sanka was always present, when she faced troubles and mayhem.

Her thoughts wandered to the past. Unknown to her, she commenced panting. Breaking silence, Sanka said,

"We will take your leave now." In a depleted tone, which increased her sorrow. She had no other alternative except to accept their departure.

She felt shy and uncomfortable, as husband Jayarathne disliked her associating with anybody.

She felt abandoned with the demise of her younger brother.

From the beginning, the only person who shared her sorrows and happiness was him. She presumed that the brother would have known her affair with Sanka.

That was confirmed by him when he said, "Sanka is a gem of a person."

She felt proud hearing this.

But she did not discuss about Sanka any day, with her brother.

Time passed by. The only solace she had was none other than bringing up the two children well. She was a prisoner in her residence and was permitted to leave the house only with husband Jayarathne. That too was very rare. Even when she was going out to town in the vehicle driven by a temporary driver, Jayarathne frequently called her on the mobile phone to ascertain details. This bothered and caused immense suffering on her.

On such instances, she inquired herself as to why Jayarathne was trying to protect her so much. It came to her mind that Jayarathne is 15 years older than her and he may fear that she will leave him forever.

There was no decrease of his arrogance and beating on her.

At times, she faced his brutal sexual assaults. Against her willingness, she had to consent to his needs. She suffered from hypertension due to this.

Though he was her husband, she despised him. Such behavior was unbearable to her. But there was no alternate solution.

The well grown up two children saw and heard all these. At time they told her, "Mother, without informing, let us go and live somewhere else."

Well aware of husband's ways, she avoided such action. Pacifying the children, she did not react.

On several occasions, he got well-dressed to go out and did not return home for several days.

Inquiring about his journey was taboo for her.

One day, discovering a lady hand bag inside his vehicle and her inquiring of same ended up with split lips, after a beating he gave her.

Another day, when inquired of a condom found inside the pockets of his trousers, it resulted her having to kneel down until he ordered otherwise.

She had to face humanly unacceptable torture by any standards.

At times, she decided to solicit advises of a lawyer for a divorce and live separately. But instantly dismissed same as she was even frightened to think about it.

Threatening, he would say, "You do not think of leaving me. If you do so, I will come in search of you and kill you." These threats made her more fearful of him.

She was frightened of the consequences that will have to be faced not only by her, but also the children.

With much reluctance, she decided to face this sorrowful life.

At times, Sanka came to her mind. Mentally, she suffered thinking of him, which was the initial chapter of her life. She recalled how depressed she was being unable to convey her love to Sanka. Every day, she loved him, though she did not convey same to him any day.

Thinking at night, day after day, she envied her youthful life already spent. However, during the day she indulged in religious activities.

❖

One Sunday at noon, as if in a dream, she heard an explosion coming from her garden, Ayanthi, alarmed, preparing lunch in the pantry ran to the garden to check the source of the explosion.

As a habit, Jayarathne often used to sit in the garden and enjoy drinking alcohol alone when his colleagues were not around.

The target of the hunter had landed accurately.

In a frenzy, Ayanthi ran towards Jayarathne. As if in a dream, she saw Jayarathne on the ground wreathing in pain with burnt and bleeding wounds. She could not fathom what had happened. She felt faintish running towards him.

From the crowd gathered around, somebody said,

"A patrol bomb had been thrown here." As if in a trance, Ayanthi tried to visualize the tragic scene.

Neighbor Kamala, wife of Bertie, seated beside Ayanthi, pacified her by rubbing her head.

Kamala said,

"These things do happen, Ayanthi. People who live by the sword die by the sword." Ayanthi felt her head swirling with a heavy load.

She had long ago realized that retribution will follow due to Jayarathne's unethical business deals, association with unreliable friends and notorious women. But, she never anticipated this to happen so soon.

She spotted him again – Sanka.

He was shouldering the coffin of Jayarathne and walked towards the cemetery along with other villagers.

Ayanthi saw this as in a dream. She wept and cried out loudly inside her. This, she realized, was not because of the demise of Jayarathne. As Sanka appeared everywhere, every time when she was in a great sorrow.

Age catching up to her and making her feeble, at times she went to the garden and stared at the sky, murmuring,

"Eldest son did not communicate for a long time." That was Sandun, who migrated to Italy after his father's death.

Sandun loved his stepmother more than his own father. Been disgusted with his father's unethical life style, he informed Ayanthi that he was leaving Sri Lanka for good, never to return.

She recalled the days of her first marriage to Aruna, throughout her entire life she will remember Aruna as he was the father of their child as well as a peace-loving husband and a shadow to her.

The third phase, being the married life with Jayarathne, was full of sorrow for her entire life. Although she had all the comforts, she spent her life as a prisoner, which she hated.

Not having animosity or speak ill of anybody, in her own conscience, she hated Jayarathne. Whispering to herself, she would say,

Will give a call to the youngest son, Dulshan. Do not know why he did not come here last weekend?

He was employed as a manager of a cyber-security company in Colombo. Apart from monthly visits to see his mother, he frequently telephoned to inquired about his mother's wellbeing.

But she dismissed the idea of calling him as he may be busy.

Sometimes, she used to do a self-assessment of the many aspects of the three phases of her triangular life.

She clearly understood that the three phases of the triangle were not similar and that one phase of the three was longer than the other two.

That was attributed to Sanka.

She realized that first phase of the life which was related to life of Sanka was well stable. It was romantic and was never expressed the love and affection practically.

In her own conscience, she still loved him secretly, seeking his love.

Tormented by her thoughts, at times she visualized her first lover's visit. A faint smile appeared on her face and she murmured,

Oh,

Sanka is coming...

END

Printed in the USA
CPSIA information can be obtained
at www.ICGtesting.com
LVHW051233221123
764524LV00067B/2674